Willie's Birthday

A Viking Easy-to-Read

You are invited to: a birthday party for Willie. Please bring your pet.

Story by **Anastasia Suen**

Illustrations by **Allan Eitzen**

Based on the characters created by

Ezra Jack Keats

VIKING

NEWFIELD

VIKING
Published by the Penguin Group
Penguin Putnam Books for Young Readers,
345 Hudson Street, New York, New York 10014, U.S.A.
Penguin Books Ltd, 27 Wrights Lane, London W8 5TZ, England
Penguin Books Australia Ltd, Ringwood, Victoria, Australia
Penguin Books Canada Ltd, 10 Alcorn Avenue, Toronto, Ontario, Canada M4V 3B2
Penguin Books (N.Z.) Ltd, 182-190 Wairau Road, Auckland 10, New Zealand

Penguin Books Ltd, Registered Offices: Harmondsworth, Middlesex, England

First published in 2001 by Viking,
a division of Penguin Putnam Books for Young Readers.

1 3 5 7 9 10 8 6 4 2

Copyright © Ezra Jack Keats Foundation, 2001
All rights reserved
Text by Anastasia Suen
Illustrations by Allan Eitzen

LIBRARY OF CONGRESS CATALOGING-IN-PUBLICATION DATA
Suen, Anastasia.
Willie's birthday / story by Anastasia Suen ; illustrations by Allan
Eitzen ; based on the characters created by Ezra Jack Keats.
p. cm.
Summary: A "Bring Your Pet" birthday party gets out of hand when the
pets show more interest in chasing each other than in celebrating.
ISBN 0-670-88943-1
[1. Dogs—Fiction. 2. Pets—Fiction. 3. Birthdays—Fiction.]
I. Eitzen, Allan, ill. II. Keats, Ezra Jack. III. Title.
PZ7.S94343 Wi 2001
[E]—dc21
00-009734

Printed in Hong Kong
Set in Bookman

Viking® and Easy-to-Read® are registered trademarks of Penguin Putnam Inc.

Reading Level: 1.8

Willie's Birthday

It was Willie's birthday.

He sat and stared at the door.

"When will the party start?" asked Susie.

"As soon as everyone gets here," said Peter.

He put the birthday cake on the table.

Ding dong!

Arf! Arf! barked Willie.

"Hooray!" said Susie. "They're here!"

"Are you ready, birthday boy?"
asked Peter.

"Happy birthday, Willie," said Archie.

"Happy birthday, Willie," said Amy.

Willie wagged his tail at them.

"This is for you, Willie," said Archie.

He put a present on the floor.

"Here's another one, Willie," said Amy.

Willie sniffed the presents.

He pulled on the ribbon.

"Not yet!" said Peter.

Peter put the presents on the table.

Arf! Arf! barked Willie.

He ran in circles around the table.

Meow! went Archie's cat.

She jumped on the couch.

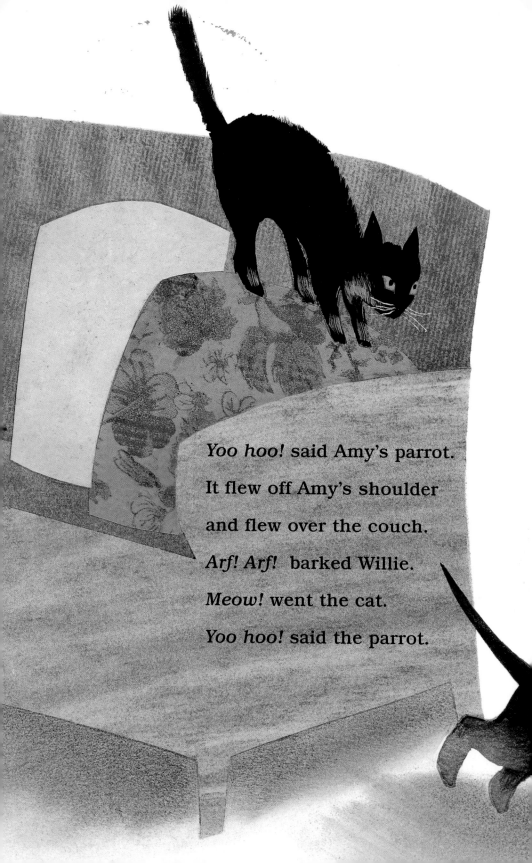

Yoo hoo! said Amy's parrot.
It flew off Amy's shoulder
and flew over the couch.
Arf! Arf! barked Willie.
Meow! went the cat.
Yoo hoo! said the parrot.

"Come here, silly Willie," said Peter.

"Yes," said Susie, "it's time for party hats."

She gave Peter, Archie, and Amy a hat.

"Can your cat wear a hat?" asked Susie.

"I don't know," said Archie, "but we can try.

"I'll hold the cat, you put on the hat," he said.

"Hooray!" said Susie.

She put the hat on the cat, but . . .

Meow!

The cat hit the hat with her paw.

She jumped out of Archie's arms.

Yoo hoo!

Amy's parrot flew down and picked

up the hat.

Then the parrot flew away.

Arf! Arf!

Willie ran after the parrot.

The cat jumped onto the table.

Water sloshed out of the fishbowl.

Meow! purred the cat.

"My fish!" said Susie. "Shoo! Go away!"

Archie took the cat off the table.

"It's not time to eat," said Archie.

Amy whistled.

The parrot flew back and

landed on her shoulder.

"Come here, silly Willie," said Peter.

"Let's play a game."

"What kind of game?" asked Archie.

"Pin the tail on the dog?"

Arf! Arf!

"No one will pin you, Willie," said Peter.

"He already has a tail," said Susie. "See?"

"So what is the game?" asked Archie.

"Give the dog a bone," said Peter.

"A *paper* bone," said Susie.

Everyone laughed.

"Can I put the blindfold on Willie?"

asked Susie.

"Okay," said Peter.

Willie licked Peter's face.

"Hold still, silly Willie," said Peter.

"I can't tie it," said Susie.

"Let me help," said Amy.

Yoo hoo!

Amy's parrot flew off her shoulder.

Arf! Arf!

Willie wiggled and barked at the parrot.

The cat hissed and jumped on the table.

Meow! purred the cat.

She put her paw into the fishbowl.

"My fish!" said Susie.

She let go of the blindfold.

"Shoo! Shoo! Go away!"

Willie jumped out of Peter's arms.

Arf! Arf! he barked.

Meow! went the cat.

Peter picked up the fishbowl.

"Safe!" he said.

Willie grabbed the tablecloth, and pulled.

The cat jumped off the table . . .

and the cake fell on the floor.

"Willie!" said Peter.

He put the fishbowl back on the table.

Everyone looked at the cake.

"What will we do?" asked Susie.

Peter looked at Willie.

"Come here, birthday boy," he said.

"We can still eat the cake," said Peter.

"But it fell over," said Susie.

"Only part of the cake is smashed,"
said Peter.

"We can give some of that to Willie."

Arf! Arf!

Everyone laughed.

Peter cut the cake.

He gave Willie the first piece.

"Happy birthday, silly Willie!"